Wishing you all the best,
... me to
... loving
... rah

Welcome to the world
little one! You have
an amazing mother
Wishing you all the
best! ♡
—Larisa

TO Baby

FROM

Liz Ashlee
Larisa & Sarah!
—Foothill BH

Welcome Baby ♡
You are so
loved! And
so lucky to
have a superhero
for a mom!
—Ashlee

Baby and
family — Have
a wonderful
life!
—Liz B
FH BH

HOORAY FOR YOU!

sourcebooks
jabberwocky

Marianne Richmond

For quite a long time, the world

SAVED A PLACE.

Millions were born,
yet none filled
YOUR
SPACE.

Until the second of a minute of
ONE SPECIAL DAY,

you took your first breath

and the world said,

"HOORAY!"

Perfectly timed, not one minute more,
you
suddenly were where you were not before.

But planning preceded your earthly debut as

ALL

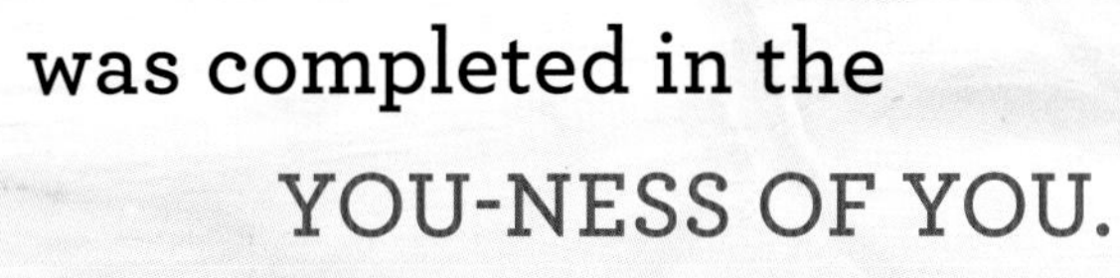

was completed in the

YOU-NESS OF YOU.

"YOU-NESS?"

you ask. Quite hard to describe,
it's your STYLE OF BEING,
your rhythm or vibe.

It's the GRAND SUM of you that sets you apart.

Your body and brains, plus your

SPIRIT AND HEART.

Isn't it something that

is not like another in the WHOLE HUMAN RACE?

Your SMILE,

for starters, curves up just so
when you LAUGH or act silly
or tell jokes that you know.

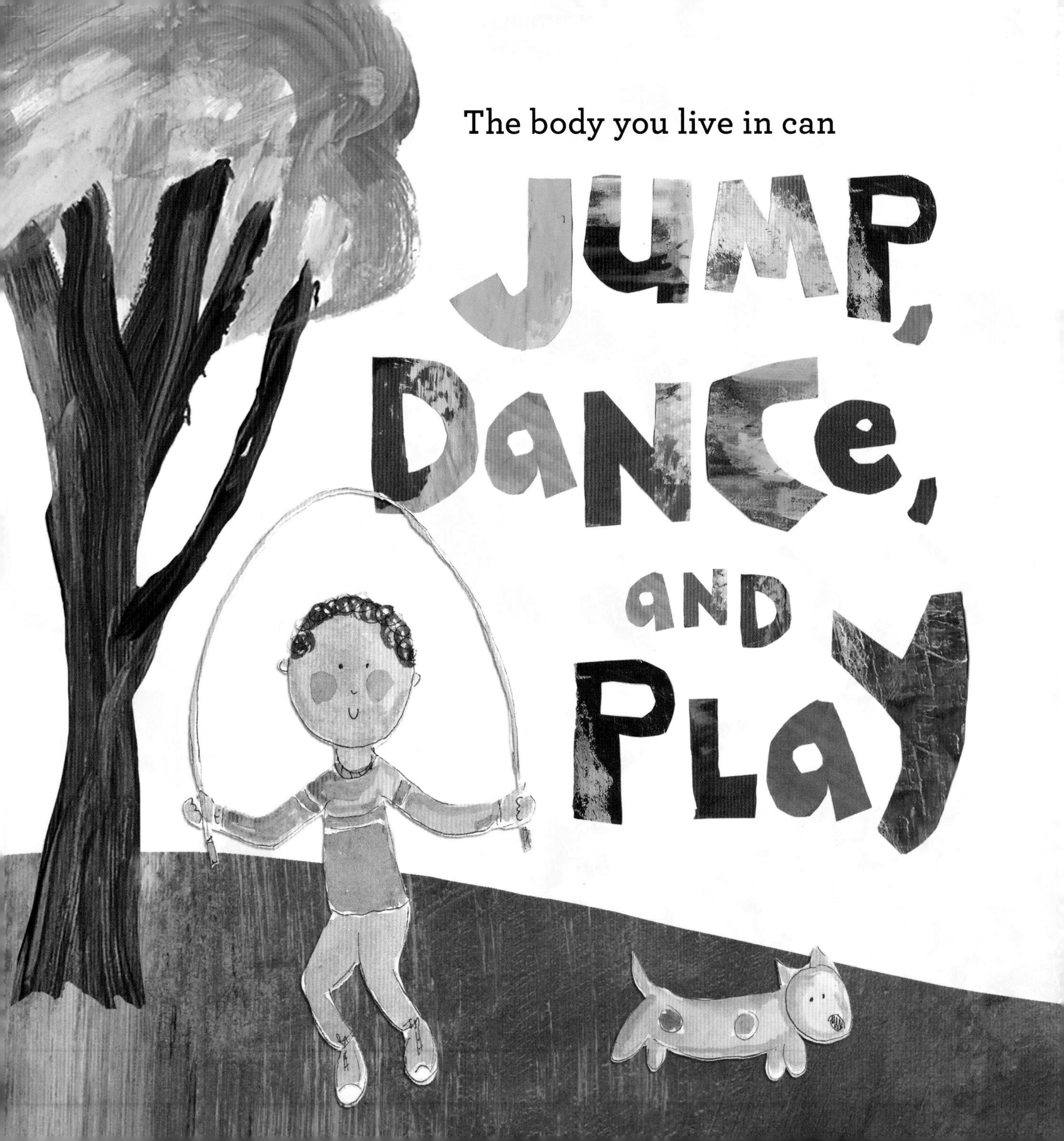
The body you live in can
JUMP,
DANCE,
AND
PLAY

with custom-built parts to move
YOUR
OWN
WAY.

Even your

HAIR,

be it black, brown, or red,

does its

OWN

THING

on top of your head!

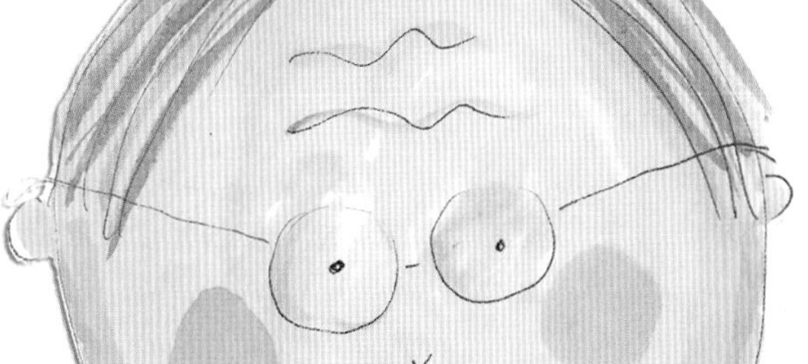

And your certain good looks
are just one teensy part
of the you-ness galore of your

MIND

and your

HEART.

This is the essence of what you're about,

within and throughout.

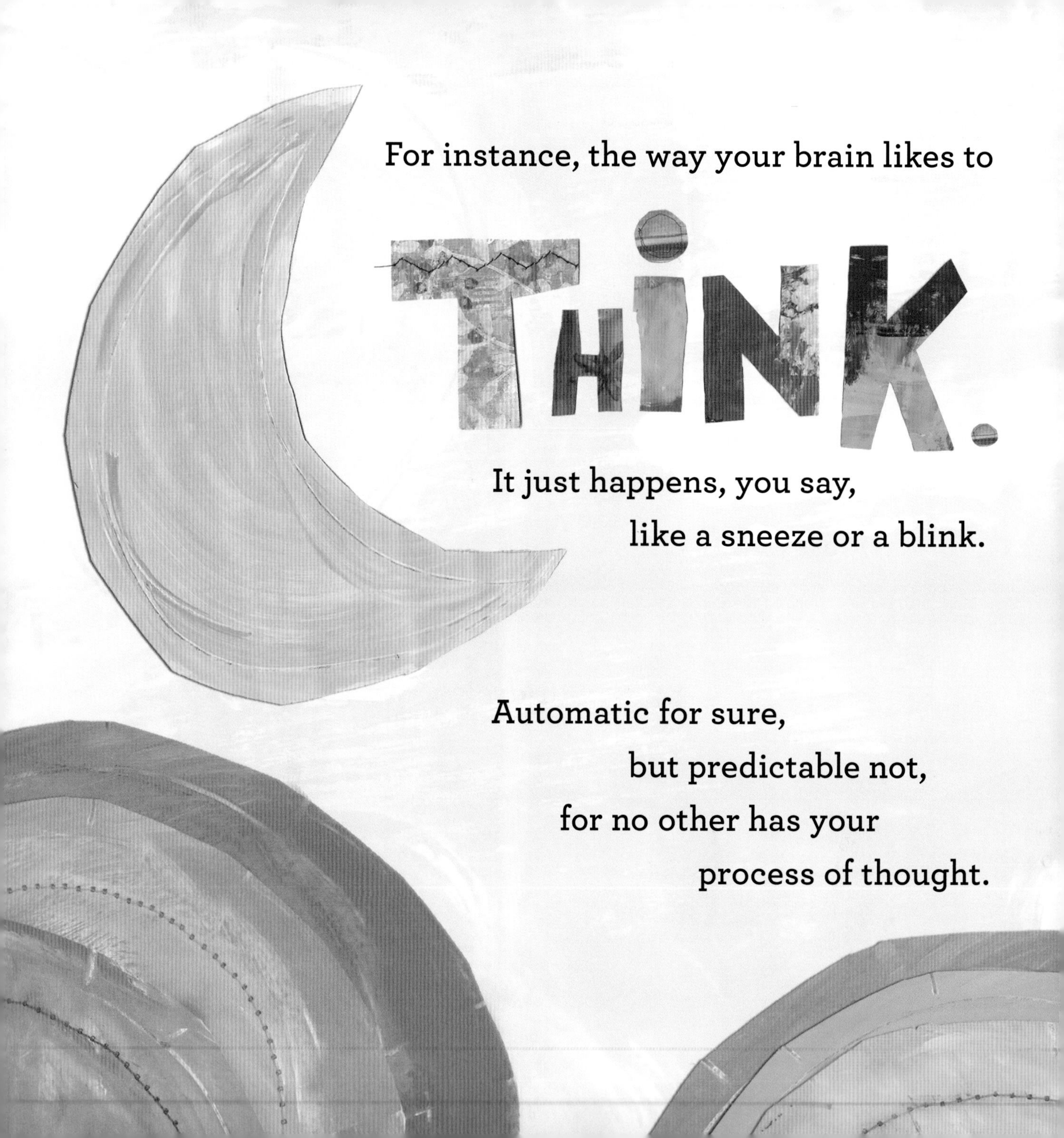

For instance, the way your brain likes to

THINK.

It just happens, you say,
like a sneeze or a blink.

Automatic for sure,
but predictable not,
for no other has your
process of thought.

You think

and original schemes.

Your wide-eyed

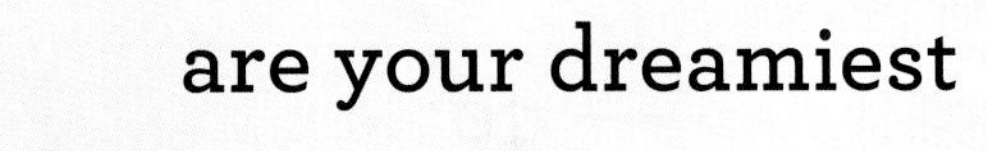

are your dreamiest

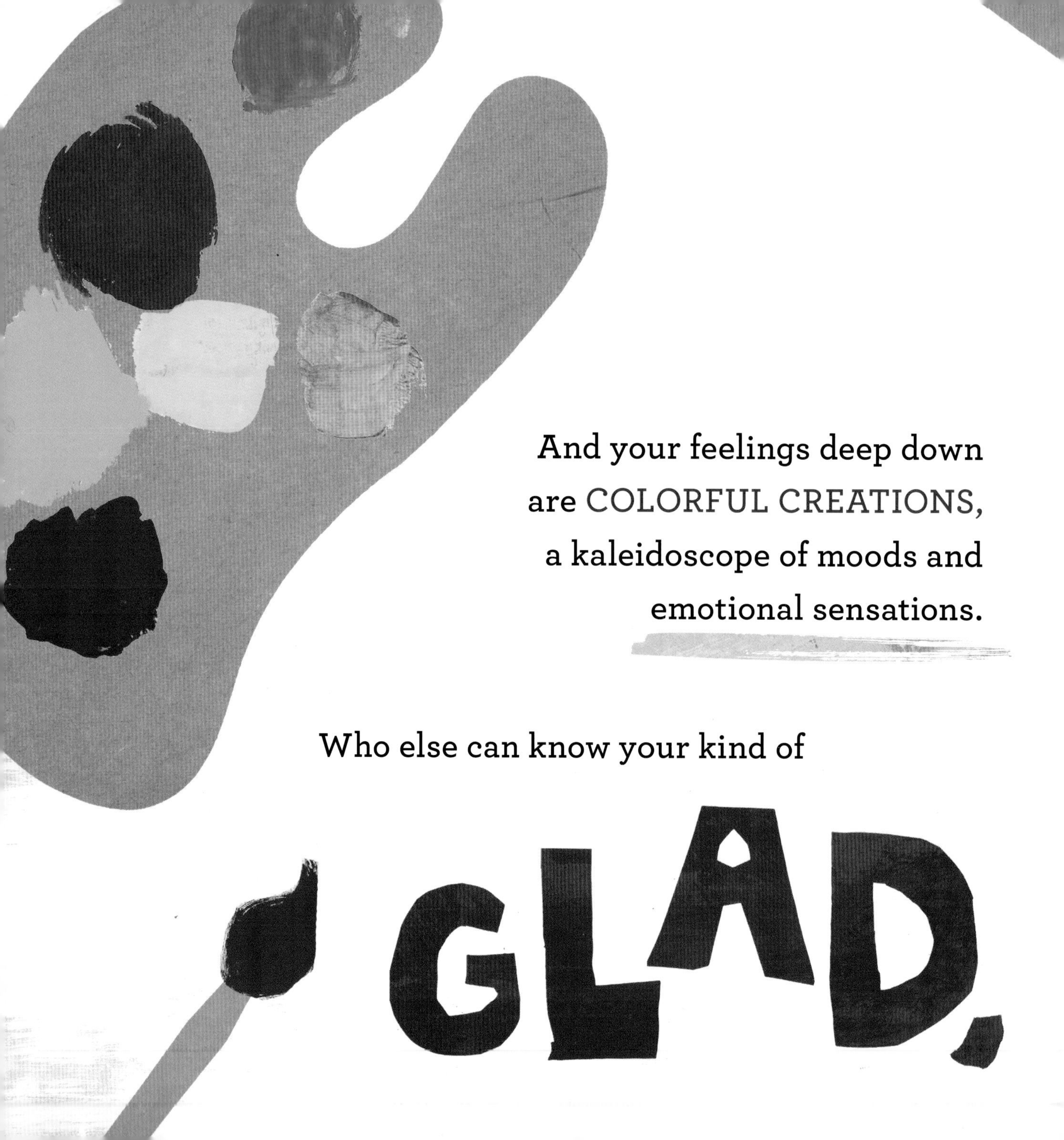

And your feelings deep down
are COLORFUL CREATIONS,
a kaleidoscope of moods and
emotional sensations.

Who else can know your kind of

GLAD,

SILLY,
EXCITED,
GRUMPY,
OR SAD.

And the cool thing
that's true is how you can

GROW

when there's thinking
to CHANGE
or new stuff to know.

YOU'RE PERFECT AS YOU,

but my friend, you will see
days when delighted is
NOT what you'll be.

And you might even think,
“I’d sure wish to be
like him, her, or them.
Any person but
ME!”

Then stop that at once.
Put
GLOOM
on the shelf.

Say “Goodbye doubt” and
“HOORAY SELF!”

Yes, from head to toe tip, you're truly

ORIGINAL,

a creation in progress,

a distinct individual.

Look the world over
and you'll never find
a duplicate of you-ness
that's your
ONE
OF A
KIND!

On the day you were born,

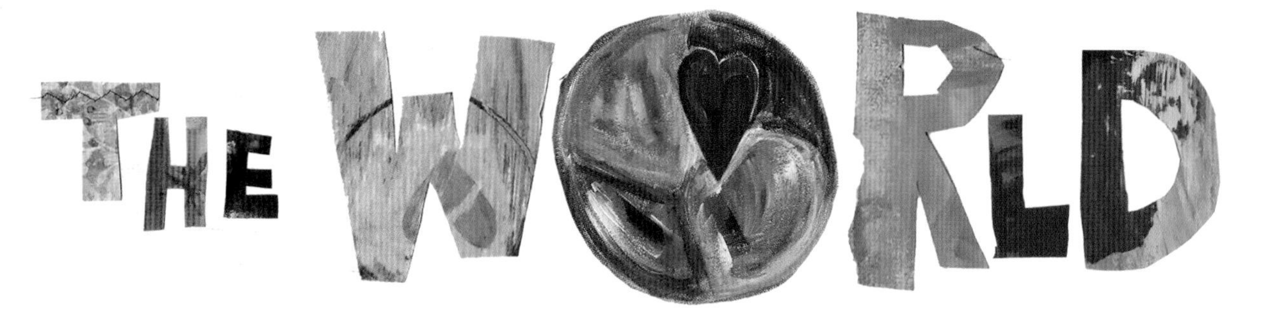

grew by one, a life with BIG PURPOSE and much to be done.

Look in the mirror.

Stand tall. Smile BIG.

Shout,

"HOORAY FOR ME!"

MARIANNE RICHMOND is a bestselling author and artist who has touched the lives of millions for more than two decades by creating books that celebrate the love of family. Visit her at mariannerichmond.com.

"My books help you share your heart and connect with those you love."

Published by Sourcebooks Jabberwocky, an imprint of Sourcebooks, Inc.
P.O. Box 4410, Naperville, Illinois 60567-4410
(630) 961-3900
Fax: (630) 961-2168
sourcebooks.com

Library of Congress Cataloging-in-Publication Data is on file with the publisher.

Source of Production: PrintPlus Limited, Shenzhen, Guangdong Province, China
Date of Production: May 2019
Run Number: 5015330

Printed and bound in China.
PP 10 9 8 7 6 5 4 3 2